for Alice

A is for Arabia.
This alphabet will tell
Of the Arabs and their customs
And the lands in which they dwell.

B is for bedouin
Walking through the sand,
A falcon on his arm,
A stick in his hand.

C is for camel
In training for the race,
Being fed on milk and honey –
Do you think she'll take first place?

D is for dhow
Sailing on the sea.
And what's that in the hold?
Good gracious! A T.V!

E is for Eid.
Can you see the moon?
Ramadan is over
And there'll be presents soon.

8

F is for fort
To protect the land from harm.
If ever the guard spied trouble
He would sound the alarm.

G is for gold.
Look at all those rings,
The pretty chains and bangles
And other sparkling things.

H is for henna.
What a lovely bride,
With painted hands and painted feet
And ladies at her side.

I is for Iftar –
The breaking of the fast
As evening falls in Ramadan
When daylight hours are past.

J is for jebel.
Jameela climbs up high,
The air is cool and clear up here.
Can she touch the sky?

K is for khanjar
With its curved and shiny blade.
The sheath is worked in silver –
See how beautifully it's made.

L is for lizard
Running up the wall.
Wouldn't you like to have a go?
Be careful! You might fall!

M is for mosque
Where Muslims go to pray.
The Muezzin calls from the minaret
Five times a day.

N is for nakhuda,
The captain of the ship,
In charge of lots of divers
On another pearling trip.

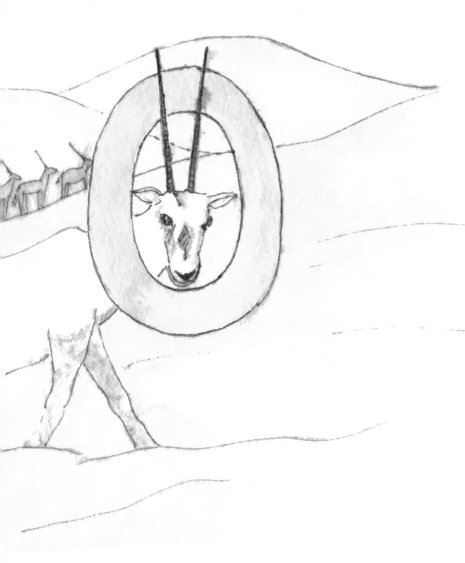

O is for oryx
With long spiral horns.
From a distance in the desert
Men thought them unicorns!

P is for palm.
See the boy climb the tree
To cut a bunch of juicy dates
To share with you and me.

Q is for Qu'ran –
Come and take a look
As Qassim reads the Word of God
From the Holy Book.

R is for Ramadan –
A month to fast and pray
When families stay up late at night
And don't eat food all day.

S is for souq.
What shall Samia buy?
See the sacks of spices
And the pots and pans piled high.

T is for tent –
Tariq lives in one,
It's made from goat hair rugs
Which protect him from the sun.

U is for umm,
The Arabic for mother –
She looks after Laila
And her little baby brother.

V is for veil
To cover a lady's face,
As she walks out in the souq
Or any public place.

W is for wadi
And when it starts to rain
As if by magic frogs appear
In rock pools once again!

X is a kiss,
And a kiss is a greeting
Used throughout the Arab world
When two good friends are meeting.

Y is for "Yallah!",
You can hear Youssef say
As he tells Yasmeen to hurry up -
"We haven't got all day!"

Z is for zakat –
Giving money to the poor.
It's the fifth pillar of Islam
And a part of Muslim law.

Other children's titles from
STACEY INTERNATIONAL

The Children's Encyclopaedia of Arabia
Mary Beardwood

Price: £ 19.95
ISBN: 1 900988 33X

Elvis the Camel
Barbara Devine
Illustrated by Patricia Al Fakhri

Price: £ 9.50
ISBN: 1 900988 399

Fizza the Flamingo
Marilyn Sheffield
Illustrated by Patricia Al Fakhri

Price: £ 4.50
ISBN: 1 900988 631

One Humpy Grumpy Camel
Julia Johnson
Illustrated by Emily Styles

Price: £ 7.99
ISBN: 1 900988 755

The Pearl Diver
Julia Johnson
Illustrated by Patricia Al Fakhri

Price: £ 9.99
ISBN: 1 900988 585

The Cheetah's Tale
Julia Johnson
Illustrated by Susan Keeble

Price: £12.50
ISBN: 1 900988 879

A Gift of the Sands
Julia Johnson
Illustrated by Emily Styles

Price: £12.50
ISBN: 1 900988 917